DANCING
FEATHERS

DANCING FEATHERS

by

Christel Kleitsch and Paul Stephens

ANNICK PRESS LTD.

Annick Press Ltd. gratefully acknowledges the
contributions of The Canada Council and The
Ontario Arts Council

Canadian Cataloguing in Publication Data

Kleitsch, Christel.
  Dancing feathers

(Spirit Bay)
Based on the movie Dancing Feathers, by Spirit
Bay Productions.
ISBN 0-920303-25-0 (pbk.).

1. Indians of North America—Canada—Juvenile
fiction. I. Stephens, Paul. II. Ense, Don.
III. Title. IV. Series.

PS8571.L44D35 1985   jC813'.54   C84-099775-2
PZ7.K58Da 1985

Cover Design by Helmut Weyerstrahs
Photos courtesy Spirit Bay Productions

Distributed in Canada by:
Annick Educational
15 Patricia Avenue
Willowdale, Ontario
M2M 1H9

Printed and bound in Canada

My Two Boys—
AAJ and NK

Spirit Bay is where I live and I'll bet you've never been to any place like it in your whole life. The first thing you'd notice if you came to visit, is that it's small, really small. Only about forty houses. The second thing you'd probably notice is that almost everybody here is Indian. That's because Spirit Bay is an Ojibway reserve. I know how to speak Ojibway too, but mostly I speak English.

If you saw my house you might think it's kind of run-down (my father hates repairs and painting and stuff), but inside it's really cozy. There's only two kids in my family—me and my older brother Minnow. Minnow's his nickname—he'd kill me if I told you his real name. (The only hint I'll give is that it starts with an 'R' and there's a song about a reindeer with his name.) Besides me and Minnow, there's our father, Baba, and Gok'mis, our grandmother. And that's everybody. My mother, she died when I was little.

Oh, I guess I haven't even told you my name yet. Hi, I'm Tafia—Tafia Shebagabow. (Bet you can't say that five times in a row really fast!) You probably want to know something about me too. Well....I'm eleven years old and I'm in grade five and my favourite subject is art. My best friend is Mavis. My Gok'mis calls us Dog and Bone 'cause Mave is always running around yapping like a little dog, and I'm Bone, kind of stubborn and quiet. We make a good combination, most of the time anyway. What else should I tell you about myself...? I can't think of anything right now, and besides, you'll find out lots more about me pretty soon.

You might think that life around here is kind of dull, us being way up in northern Ontario, far away from big cities and everything. (Thunder Bay is the closest and it's about a three hour drive away. I've been there five times now.) But we find lots to do. For one thing, everybody knows everybody here, and people visit a lot. And Spirit Bay is right on a big lake—Lake Nipigon. That's where we swim and fish and harvest wild rice. And all around is the bush. Miles and miles and miles of it. That's where we hunt and trap and look for berries and stuff.

Believe it or not, sometimes some pretty exciting things happen to me. Like one time last summer—I sure got myself in a lot of trouble....

CHAPTER ONE

"Pick up two." Mavis slapped down a card. "Miss your turn." She slapped down another one. "Pick up two." Another card. "Miss your turn." And another—an eight of hearts this time.

"Oh no!" I moaned. "Ma-a-a-ve!"

She paused to think for a moment. "Ummm. ... I make it diamonds. *Last card*!"

Last card! My only chance now was to change it from diamonds. I looked down at my hand that was overflowing. A million cards—but not one single eight!

Mavis giggled, covering her mouth with the one card left in her hand. "I'm going to win again, Tafia."

Only one thing to do. I reached over and picked up a card. "YAY!!" I shrieked, tossing it on top of the pile. It was an eight! "I make it hearts!"

Mave groaned and fell backwards on the bed. "You dirty rat!" Then she slowly got up and dropped her card onto the pile. It was a heart! I couldn't believe it.

"Fooled you!" she said. "You thought I had a diamond, didn't you?"

I sure did—who'd be crazy enough to make it diamonds when all she had left was a heart? How can you beat somebody who plays like that? That Mavis!

She couldn't stop laughing while she was adding up the points. "You're only losing by two hundred and fifteen points—you could still win."

"Are you kidding?" I gathered up the cards.

"You don't want to play anymore?"

"It's almost supper anyway," I said, "and Aunt Lily'll be here any minute. Let's go bug my brother till she comes."

Of course Minnow was watching baseball. Wearing his Blue Jay's cap—naturally.

He grinned as soon as he saw me. "How much did you lose by this time, Tafia?"

"She didn't, she won," Mave said flopping down onto the couch. That's what I like about Mavis—she sticks up for you. "What's the score?" she asked.

"The Jays are losing," Minnow said in a disgusted voice.

"Well, I figured that. But what's the score?" Mavis is an Expos fan. They always fight about baseball when she comes over.

Just then I heard the back door open in the kitchen and Aunt Lily talking to Baba and Gok'mis. She sure sounded excited about something.

"Are you sure you don't want to come, Mama? It's in two weeks and—" she was saying as we came in.

"Hi, Aunt Lily," I said. "What's in two weeks?"

"Wouldn't you like to know, nosy!" Aunt Lily teased crinkling up her eyes in a smile. "Do you think I should tell her, George?" she asked Baba.

Baba pretended to think it over carefully. "Well...I don't know," he finally said. "Maybe you should wait till after supper...or even next week. There's lots of time—"

"C'mon, what're you talking about?"

Aunt Lily looked at me with a smile. "Lots of time."

Well, something was sure going on. And I guessed that I was in it too from the way Aunt Lily and Baba were acting. But what?

Just looking at them I knew I wasn't going to get any answers, and Gok'mis wasn't saying anything either, so I started setting the table with Mavis.

Aunt Lily watched us for about a minute, then

she said, "Well, if you don't want to hear about the powwow and going to Toronto..."

I knew it! I knew she'd tell if I stopped asking. Aunt Lily is like a little kid when she's got a secret—she just can't wait to tell.

"What powwow?" "Going to Toronto?" Mavis and I asked both together.

So Aunt Lily told us how she was planning to go down to Toronto to sell her paintings (she's an artist), and after, she was going to a big powwow at Curved Lake. "Do you want to come, Tafia?" she asked me.

"Toronto! Sure!" I said.

"And what about you, Mavis?" Aunt Lily added. "Gok'mis says it's too long a trip for her, so I've got room for one more in my truck. If you want to ask your parents—"

"Oh, yeah! I'll ask them. Great! Wow, a powwow!" Mave babbled as she ran out the back door. You don't have to ask her twice about a thing like that.

I was pretty excited myself. Me and Mave down in Toronto together—our very first time! The big city! And with Aunt Lily too!

"And the best part," she went on, "is that you can do your jingle dress dance at the powwow, Tafia." Before I could answer, Aunt Lily turned to Gok'mis. "What do you think? Should she do it?"

Say no, Gok'mis!! I said to myself. Say no!

Gok'mis gave me a long look and then she nodded. "When the time is right, the bird will fly."

Gok'mis talks like that a lot—in sayings. Sometimes it's hard to understand exactly what she means. But this time I knew—she was saying that I was ready. I could feel my stomach sliding right down to my toes. That darn jingle dress! I wished I'd never seen it.

I still remembered the day Gok'mis suggested making it. She was so happy and excited, and I was too. My whole life I had been watching Gok'mis dancing in hers, wearing the eagle feather in her hair. Now I would have my own.

Baba drove us over to the sewing store in Beardmore to pick out the material. It's really pretty—turquoise, my favourite colour. When the dress part was finished, I helped Gok'mis attach the jingles. It seemed like it would take forever! I counted them one time, but I forgot how many there were. Hundreds for sure. (The jingles are little metal tubes made of rolled-up snuff tin tops.) Gok'mis was saving them up for years. Ever since I was a little baby, she knew that she wanted me to have a jingle dress.

When we were finally finished and I put it on, Gok'mis just stood there looking at me, smiling and smiling. Then she held up the mirror so I could see too. I felt as though I was going to shout or cry or something. The dress was so beautiful!

Every step I took, all the jingles bounced up against each other. It was such a pretty sound—like in winter when there's freezing rain and everything is covered with ice and then the sun comes out. You stand still in the woods and everywhere you can hear the little pieces of ice melting off the trees and falling down on the hard snow crust. Tinkling like little bells all around you. That's what the jingle dress reminded me of. I loved it!

"Now I will teach you," Gok'mis had said to me in Ojibway, her old voice cracking.

That's when I knew I was in trouble. It's funny, but the whole time we were making the dress, I never thought about the dancing part. Dumb, right? After all, that's what a jingle dress is for—dancing the jingle dress dance. How could I explain to Gok'mis that dancing was o.k. for the old ones, like her, but not for me? I would just feel silly. But I knew if I told her she would be really hurt, so I kept my feelings inside and let her teach me. All the time, though, I knew there was no way I was ever going to dance in public! No way!

I was busy trying to figure out how I was going to get out of this dancing mess when Mavis burst back into the kitchen all out of breath. "I can go! I can go!" she cried, hugging first Aunt Lily and then me. She was just about jumping out of her skin with excitement about the powwow and Toronto.

Toronto. Yeah, what about Toronto? I always wanted to see it. But I was positive Aunt Lily wouldn't take me if I refused to dance.

"—maybe we'll even see movie stars and a base-

17

ball game and oh, wow, we can go to the—" Mavis was still going on and on.

"So what do you say, Tafia? You going to dance for everybody?" Baba asked me.

I sure wasn't going to give up Toronto. I would just have to take the bad with the good. "Yes," I said.

It was all decided. I was going to Toronto and I was dancing at the powwow.

Playing cards wasn't the only thing I was unlucky about, I thought that night before I went to sleep. But maybe if I was smart, like Mavis at Crazy Eights, I could figure some way of getting out of the dancing. Yeah, maybe....

CHAPTER TWO

I woke up early the morning we were leaving on our trip. It wasn't even really light out yet but I couldn't stay in bed one more second, so I pulled on my clothes and tiptoed out of the house. All of Spirit Bay was still asleep. It was a good time for thinking things over.

When I got to the bay the sun was coming up over the tops of the trees. The sky was changing slowly from grey to blue. I sat down and lowered my bare feet slowly into the water. Brrr! It was still cool from the night.

A soft wind was moving across the surface of the bay, ruffling up lots of little waves. They caught bits of sunlight that flashed in my eyes.

I noticed then that I wasn't the first one up that morning. There was a big eagle high in the sky over my head. He wasn't really flying, just kind of floating round and round in circles, smooth and lazy. He made it look so easy. No wonder people a long time ago thought that they could fly if they just attached big wings to their arms.

"Hey, eagle!" I yelled up to him. "What are you doing?" I knew the answer—hunting. Wild animals, that's what they're always doing—hunting, looking for food.

In a way, you know, life is simple for them. They only have one thing to do. They don't have to make decisions when they wake up in the morning. You can bet no eagle ever asked himself, "Should I go to the powwow and do my jingle dress dance, or should I go hide out somewhere?" No sir, you can bet your life he didn't! Eagles, they just go out and do their job.

But for me, Tafia Shebagabow, things aren't always that easy.

I shivered in the cool morning air. I wished that I was back home sleeping in my warm bed instead of out here on the dock. But that's how it always is when I'm worried. Some people, like Minnow, chew their fingernails down to nothing. Other people, like me, get up too early in the morning and go down to the bay and watch the water.

I felt small. Small and scared. And mad too. Mad at myself for getting into this.

I got up and did a few steps of my dance, but it was no good. I was clumsy as a bear cub. Who would want to see me dance? Nobody, that's who!

Just then I heard a squealing of tires. It was my uncle Cheemo in his beat-up old red truck coming up the road toward the dock. As usual he was going too fast, kicking up gravel and dust behind him.

When he spotted me, he leaned out the window and started waving and yelling. "Hey there, Tafia! Hey!" Cheemo has a very loud voice.

When I was little, I remember I used to be scared of Cheemo because he was big and his voice was so loud. He always would pick me up and toss me in the air. I didn't like it much. Now I'm used to him more and he's o.k. He's always joking around, teasing, making people laugh.

Cheemo's buddy, Hawkno, was with him. They were both wearing old fishing clothes and orange caps. They looked like twins except Cheemo is fat and Hawkno is skinny. Right away Cheemo started tickling me—as usual! I think I'm getting too big for that stuff, but Cheemo doesn't. "Stop! Stop!" I squawked.

"How ya doing?" Hawkno asked me. He was loading their fishing gear into Cheemo's boat.

I shrugged. "O.k...."

"What do you mean—o.k.?" Cheemo yelled.

"O.k....just o.k." I didn't know what else to say.

"I've never heard anything so silly, have you

Hawkno? This little girl is going to be the hit of the powwow, and she says 'just o.k.'!"

How do you know, Cheemo? I thought. How do you know I won't be awful?

Hawkno started up the motor. "Come on, Cheemo. Let's go."

Cheemo nodded and threw his jacket into the boat. "So, when are you leaving, Tafia?"

"Soon. This morning. You're going too, aren't you....Saturday?"

Cheemo grinned. "Maybe. Just maybe... Hey, Lily still going to Toronto first?"

"Yeah."

"Well, you have fun now, you hear. And don't you two girls give Aunt Lily a hard time, eh?" He winked at me. "No stealing cars this time!"

I started to laugh. "Cheemo, you're crazy!"

"Crazy?" He pretended to look mad and started to get out of the boat again, but Hawkno gunned the motor just in time. "I'll get you, you'll see," Cheemo shouted.

I laughed and waved good-bye until the boat got small. Cheemo *is* crazy, too, you know. Funny crazy, I mean. He made me feel good for a few minutes, but then the bad feeling started coming back.

I decided to go home. Everybody would be getting up now and it was time to get ready to leave.

That eagle was still up there circling in the sky. He made me think of the eagle feather Gok'mis wears in her headdress when she dances.

"When the time is right, the bird will fly," Gok'mis had said. Well eagle, I thought, the time will never be right for me to dance. Never.

CHAPTER THREE

At home Gok'mis was making tea for herself while Baba finished breakfast. For them it was just a day like any other.

Baba gave me a big smile. "You're up early today, *danis*."

Just then there was a loud yelp from the direction of the bathroom. Baba laughed. "Minnow must be shaving again. Third time this year." He called out, "Don't slit your throat!"

A few seconds later Minnow stumbled in half-asleep, bits of bloody toilet paper stuck on his chin and cheeks. Also his baseball shirt was on backward... and inside out. Minnow in the morning!

"Up early practising, eh Tafia?" he said sitting down at the table. "You sure need it."

"You mind your own business!" I snapped, my voice going louder than I meant it to. I wasn't in the mood for any more teasing. Minnow didn't notice, he just kept stuffing bannock into his mouth. But

Gok'mis did. She shot me a quick glance over her shoulder. That Gok'mis—she notices everything!

I'll try to tell you about Gok'mis. If you look at her, the first thing you think is that she's really old. Her face is covered with millions of wrinkles like soft leather. She doesn't say much, she never asks you any questions, but I think that's because she already knows the answers. When I was little I used to think that she could look through walls to see what I was doing. Now I'm not little any more, but I'm still not sure.

That morning I was afraid of Gok'mis—afraid that if she looked at me too long she would see the secret in my heart.

"Aren't you having any breakfast?" Baba asked me.

"I'm not hungry right now," I answered.

"You starting to get the jitters about dancing at the powwow?"

I shrugged. "Yeah, I guess. Anyway, I have to finish packing my stuff." And I took off down the hallway to my room.

There was only one thing left to put into my knapsack—the jingle dress. I had saved it for last so it wouldn't get so creased. I took it out of the closet and laid it down on my bed. The jingles clattered and rattled. "Quiet!" I thought, "you trouble-maker!" and I grabbed it and stuffed it into my bag.

At that minute I hated that jingle dress more than I'd ever hated anything. How was I going to get up and dance in front of all those people at the pow-wow? I couldn't do it! I couldn't!! If only I never had to see that stupid dress ever again!

And then I got my idea. It happened so fast—the idea and doing it both seemed to come in the very same second. I took out the dress, opened my closet, stuck it under a pile of dirty laundry on the floor and shut the closet tight. Then I tied up my bag and ran out of the room.

When I got to the kitchen, Baba was by the door putting on his boots getting ready to leave for work. Gok'mis was standing at the sink with her back to me. She hadn't left the room, but still I expected her to turn around and say, "Tafia, your dress, why don't you have it?" But the seconds ticked by and she didn't.

All I wanted to do was get out of there. "I'm ready," I said to Baba. My voice was shaking but somehow I got the words out.

"I'll walk you to Mavis', o.k.?" he said.

I just nodded.

I started to head for the door but Gok'mis' voice stopped me. "Tafia?" she said softly.

But she only wanted to kiss me good-bye. I ran over and hugged her and then I was out the door with Baba. Made it! I was so relieved I didn't hear a word he said all the way over to Mave's house.

I could hardly believe what I had just done. Me, Tafia, who always thinks about everything at least five times before she does it. It was too crazy! What was I going to do when I got to the powwow with no jingle dress? There was no time to think about that now. I'll worry about it later, I said to myself.

When we got to Mave's, Baba gave me a hug. "I know you'll do great, Tafia. You'll make us all proud," he said. "And you do what your Aunt Lily tells you, o.k.? No foolin' around."

"Oh Baba . . . !!" I said squeezing him as tight as I could. I felt like I was going to cry.

"Don't you worry now, Tafia," he said, "everything will be fine. You have a good time." I nodded and then he turned and walked off down the road. As I watched him go I was kind of sick in my stomach.

Mavis was on the phone in the kitchen when I walked in. She was telling somebody about our trip. Mave's got lots of friends, not like me—I've only got her.

"Yeah, just me and Tafia and Lily," she was saying. "For sure I'm going up the CN Tower." She smiled when she saw me and waved. "Sure I'm going to the powwow too.... No, I'm not going to, but Tafia is.... I don't have a dress.... Yeah, it's going to be great!"

She was so excited about going to the powwow. I guess I would have been too if it wasn't for the dancing—but not like her. You see, I'd already been to a couple of powwows when I was little and she hadn't been to any. Mave's parents never seem to go to stuff like that.

I heard a truck out front and I figured it was Aunt Lily, but when I got there it was just Minnow and a bunch of his friends. They had come to pick up Mave's brother, Hack, on their way to a baseball tournament in Thunder Bay. Billy was there too. Mave always says he likes me. Maybe, I'm not sure.

"I hear you're gonna dance at the powwow," he said to me.

I was saved from having to answer by Mavis and her big mouth. "Of course, she is!" she said grinning from the doorway. "She'll be the best. You should see her in her costume—does she ever look cute!"

All the boys laughed and whistled and I could feel myself turning red.

Just then Aunt Lily's old green truck pulled up. Cheemo calls it the Band of Noises because it makes so much racket. When Aunt Lily turned the motor off, it still kept going for a few seconds, backfiring and sputtering away.

Minnow laughed. "Hey, Lily. You really expect to get to Toronto in that pile of junk?"

"It gets me where I'm going," Aunt Lily said. Then she winked at me. "Usually."

Mavis grabbed her duffle bag and swung it into the back of the truck. "Watch the paintings, Mavis!" Aunt Lily said and she jumped in to rearrange things.

One of Mave's new puppies waddled over sniffing at Minnow's pants. He started playing with it, making it walk on its two back legs. "Hey, lookit," he said, "it's Tafia dancing." And all the boys laughed. Aunt Lily yelled at him for teasing me.

"Toronto—here we come!" Mave yelled out the window as we roared off in the truck. I wished I felt as happy as she did.

CHAPTER FOUR

It was going to be a long drive down to Toronto—two days if nothing went wrong. Aunt Lily's truck doesn't have a radio or even a tape deck so we rolled down the windows and sang all our favourite songs as loud as we could. We couldn't drown out the Band of Noises though! Mostly we sang country and western songs. I like Willie Nelson best.

Aunt Lily taught us a new song that day. It's by Buffy Ste. Marie. I had heard it before a few times, but I never learned all the words. It goes—

"Sun is up, day is on,
Look for me, I'll be gone,
Because today's the day
I'm gonna see him again
He's an Indian cowboy in the rodeo..."

That part about the Indian cowboy sounded kind of funny to me. I guess it's 'cause on TV, you know in those old movies, the Indians are always on one side and the cowboys are on the other side and they're fighting against each other. Somebody who's an Indian *and* a cowboy—he wouldn't know whose side he was on. Maybe nobody would want him. It made me sad to think of that.

Most of the country we were driving through was pretty much the same—bush and lots of little lakes—but I never get tired of looking out the window. One place we passed, these high rocky cliffs came right down to the edge of the road. They were leaning over so much they looked like they might fall crashing down on top of us. It was kind of scary.

I liked watching Aunt Lily too, while she was driving. She's so pretty and her face is always changing. One minute she was smiling like she was thinking about a joke Cheemo told her or something, another minute she'd look serious like she was thinking about her painting. She caught me watching her a couple of times and she laughed like she was embarrassed. "What are you looking at, eh?" she asked me.

We stopped for lunch beside a little lake. Aunt Lily had some sandwiches and apples for us and Mave's mother made some raisin cookies. I was supposed to bring juice but I left so fast, I forgot, so we drank some water from the lake. Then we took

off our socks and shoes and splashed around for a
while, even Aunt Lily. Did it ever feel good.

After lunch Mavis pulled out a book she had
brought along and started reading. She really likes
Judy Blume. I think she's read *Are You There, God?
It's Me, Margaret* about five times already! Some-

times I tease her and say it should be called *Are You There, Mavis? It's Me, God.* The funny thing is though, that as soon as Mave starts reading in the car, she falls asleep in about ten minutes. It happens every time. First her eyes start to blink fast and then her head starts nodding forward and before you know it, she's sleeping like a baby.

We stopped for supper at this little restaurant beside a gas station. Pretty soon after that the sun started going down. I love watching the night come over the highway. When the headlights of the cars come on one by one, the white line shines at you brighter and brighter like it has lights under the pavement.

Then it started raining and I watched the windshield wipers slapping at the little rivers of water. The rain woke Mavis up (third nap that day!) and she started right in yapping about the powwow. Mavis is one of those people who never stop talking about the thing they've got in their mind at that moment.

"Lily," Mave asked, "did you ever go to a powwow when you were our age?"

"No," Aunt Lily answered. "The church didn't like them, so they stopped them. They stopped a lot of things in those days."

"Why did they do that?" I asked.

"I don't know, Tafia. Guess they were scared."

"Scared? Of us?" That sounded crazy to me.

"Yeah, I think so."

After that Aunt Lily didn't seem to want to talk any more, she looked like she was thinking. I was thinking too—about the church being scared of Indians and their powwows. It didn't make any sense. What was there to be scared of?

After a while Aunt Lily said, very serious, "You know, girls, when I was your age . . . I didn't want to be an Indian." Aunt Lily not want to be an Indian? I

felt like somebody was telling me that day was night and I was supposed to believe it.

"Yeah," she went on. "It was like I just wanted to forget all about the past."

I couldn't get over what Aunt Lily was saying. You see, she loves Indian things, especially the music—and the art, of course. Her paintings are mostly about stuff that happens on the reserve. Everyday things, you know, like kids playing, rice harvesting, trapping. Of course, mostly white people buy her paintings. Aunt Lily says she wants to show them the beauty of the Indian way of life.

"Lily...why didn't you want to be an Indian?" Mavis asked. Mavis is never shy about asking questions, even the hard ones.

Aunt Lily told us all about what had happened to her when she was a girl. She told us how they had come and taken her away from her family when she was ten years old and put her in a live-in school far away from home. She had cried and cried and wanted to go back but they wouldn't let her. The white kids at the school had made fun of her and made her ashamed of the way she talked and the way she looked. Even the Indian kids who lived around there teased her and the other Indian kids from the bush. They called them "fish stinkers."

"I had to stay there the whole school year," Aunt Lily said. "They didn't even send me home for holidays at Christmas. They told me it was too far!"

She said that the worst part was when she finally did get back home in June, and she felt like a stranger—like she was different from everybody else on the reserve. "And every summer after that it got worse. By the time I was in high school, I didn't even want to come back. I didn't belong in Spirit Bay any more...but you know, I found out later that I didn't belong out there either." Just like the Indian cowboy in the song, I thought. Not an Indian and not a cowboy.

"Anyway," she said, "now I'm back home and I'm happy."

I remembered something that Gok'mis is always saying. It had never really made sense to me before, but now I was starting to understand. "Birds have nests, we have our past, eh, Aunt Lily?"

She nodded. "Yeah. That's right. Gok'mis is smart.... I wish I'd listened to her more when I was young."

I guess Gok'mis means that our past is where we come from—it's like our home. It's what we come back to when we're in trouble—like Aunt Lily did, coming back to Spirit Bay and being Indian again. That's why Gok'mis is always telling me about the old ways—she wants me to have a past, to know who I am: Tafia Shebagabow—Ojibway.

Aunt Lily smiled over at me. "I'm so glad we're

going to the powwow and that you're dancing, Tafia. You know, sometimes when you've been to a powwow you can feel the drum beat inside you for two days after it's over. I love powwows!"

I thought about my bag in the back of the truck with no jingle dress in it and I didn't say a word.

CHAPTER FIVE

The second day on the road was a lot like the first, lots of talking and lots of looking out the window. Except that the truck broke down. It was late when it happened—torn fan belt—so Aunt Lily just fixed it temporarily. She said it would last us till we arrived, and it did.

The next morning, there it was right in front of my eyes—Toronto!

Mavis was the first one to spot the CN Tower. She's crazy about that thing—don't ask me why. "The tallest free-standing structure in the world," she said with a big grin. You'd think she owned the place.

We rode through miles and miles of houses and apartment buildings before we got to the part Aunt Lily called downtown. Toronto is so big! I'm telling you, Thunder Bay is *nothing* compared to Toronto. And all those cars—it wasn't even six thirty in the morning and you wouldn't believe the traffic! (Hardly any pick-up trucks though, not like up by us.)

Mave and I were driving Aunt Lily crazy asking questions about everything and telling her all the places we wanted to go. I was making a list, " . . . the Science Centre and the museum . . . and Ontario Place and—"

"The CN Tower. Don't forget about the CN Tower," Mavis said.

"Yeah, right, the CN Tower. And the zoo and—"

"Hey slow down, you guys!" Aunt Lily said. "We're only gonna be here a few days you know, not a month . . . " But we didn't pay any attention to her. We were going to do *everything*!

The old Band of Noises was starting to sound kind of cranky again by the time we found a gas station. This big fat guy came out to see what we wanted. He was really grouchy when Aunt Lily asked him for a new fan belt. While he went inside to get it, Aunt Lily decided to call her friend Monica at the art gallery to tell her that we had arrived. I hoped we'd get out of there soon. I was hungry for breakfast.

Beside the door of the station I noticed a stack of newspapers all ready to be thrown out, and right on top of them was a bunch of old comics. Mave and I sat down and started looking at them.

After a few minutes, she said, "Only a few more days to the powwow, eh. I can't wait—"

"Mave!" I barked. "Will you just shut up about the stupid powwow! I'm sick of talking about it!"

Her head snapped up from her comic and there was a hurt look on her face. I was about to say that I was sorry when all of a sudden her eyes flicked past me and she yelled, *"Hey! You!"*

There was this kid in an orange T-shirt by the truck. He had one of Aunt Lily's paintings in his hand and he was running away with it. I jumped up and started after him, Mave right behind me.

He ran zigging and zagging around the people on the sidewalk like a scared rabbit through trees, but we kept right on his trail. Then he cut down this alley full of garbage cans. He kicked a few of them over so they fell in our path, but they didn't slow us down. I'm not usually such a fast runner, but that day I was flying.

When we got to the other end of the alley we spotted him disappearing into a subway entrance. O.k., I know now it was stupid to chase him like that, us not having any idea where we were going, but I wasn't thinking about anything but getting that painting back. That kid, he blasted past the ticket booth like an out-of-control freight train and we were right on his heels. I could hear the man in the booth yelling as I went by.

A subway train was just about to leave when we got to the track. That kid ran into a car a little way down, so we dashed into one too. By that time I was so tired I could hardly breathe. My side was hurting like crazy from all that running. "When the train stops, we'll see if he gets out," I told Mavis. "I think he's in the second car down." She was all red in the face and sweaty too.

I remember thinking that this wasn't exactly the way I'd imagined my first subway ride—chasing some little crook. It was weird speeding through those dark tunnels with the walls outside so close to the train windows, and then all of a sudden a lit-up station platform popping out of nowhere. I kept thinking we'd blast right through them, but every time we'd stop. It was hard to see what was happening 'cause there were a lot of people getting on and off the train at every station, going to work I suppose. About five stations went by, but we didn't see the kid get off.

I was starting to get worried that we'd lost him, when finally at a station called Dundas I spotted him run out quick and up the stairs. Mave and I followed. Just when he was almost at the top, he turned around and looked at us. I guess he'd been hoping that he'd lost us, but there we were. That's when he dropped the painting and took off. It came slipping and bouncing down the stairs toward us. Maybe his dropping it was accidental, or maybe he did it just to get rid of us, I don't know. Anyway we had the painting back, that was the important thing.

The first thing we saw when we came out of the subway was the Eaton Centre. I recognized it from a postcard Moony, that's Minnow's girlfriend, showed me. It looked beautiful—so big and the sun shining on all those windows.

I felt really happy and excited at first, but when I looked at all those people rushing past us on the sidewalk, it hit me. They were strangers and we were lost. Completely lost. How were we ever going to find Aunt Lily in all this?

"Where are we?" Mavis asked me.

"At the Eaton Centre, right? I don't know," I said.

Mavis' voice started to sound all whiney. That's how she gets when she's nervous. "Yeah, I know, but I mean what are we going to do?"

"How am I supposed to know?" I yelled. "I've never been here before, either, you know!" I couldn't remember the last time I had yelled at Mavis, but being lost made me a little crazy. And probably I was still mad at her about before, at the garage.

She put her arm around me. "C'mon Tafia, don't be mad, eh," she said. "We gotta figure this out." That's one of the things I like best about old Mavis—she's hard to stay mad at. 'Cause she's so nice. "Do you know where Lily's friend's place is? Where we're staying . . . what's her name . . . ? Monica?"

"I'm sorry, Mave," I said. "I didn't mean it."

She smiled. "It's o.k. What about Monica? Do you know where she lives?"

I shook my head, "No, I don't."

"That's o.k., we can call her. Look, there's a phone booth right over there. I've got money." She reached into her pocket and then she made a face. "I left my wallet in the truck. You got any money?"

"No."

"Well anyway, we can look up her address and then we can walk there. We'll just ask someone where it is." Mave started to head for the phone booth, but I grabbed her arm.

"I don't know her last name. Aunt Lily always just calls her Monica."

The smile fell off Mave's face. I could almost hear it land on the sidewalk with a sad little thump. I tried to think of what else we could do. How could we find Monica? Then I remembered. "I know! What about the gallery! That's it! We could look it up in the phone book. We just have to find the Indian Art Gallery."

But there was no Indian Art Gallery. There must have been a billion names in that big fat rotten phone book, but no Indian Art Gallery. Poor Mave looked like she was ready to cry and I kind of felt like it myself by then, so I said since we were here anyway, why didn't we just go in and look around the Eaton Centre. We'd figure it out later.

So we went across the street and through the revolving door into the Eaton Centre. What a place! I guess if you've never been to Toronto you probably don't know what the Eaton Centre is. It's this huge shopping place with hundreds of stores and there's plants all over the place. Outside it's made mostly of glass, sort of like a giant greenhouse. They've got everything in there and I mean it—

everything—any kind of store you can think of and tons of restaurants and banks and movies. A person could live their whole life in there and never have to come out.

The two things I liked best were the glass elevator and the spitting fountain right near it. All the water gets sucked down the drain at the bottom and then all of a sudden it starts spitting, shooting bits of water almost right to the ceiling. And that ceiling is *high*!

We also had fun in this sunglasses store. That's all they sold—a whole store full of sunglasses!—I'm not kidding. Mave pretended that she wanted to buy some and she must have tried on about fifty different kinds before the guy kicked us out. This one pair—the lenses were shaped like hearts and they were pink and white polka-dotted. Ever cool!

It's easy to forget about your problems in a place like that, but when we got to the end of the Centre, we had nowhere to go. How could we have been so stupid to get ourselves in such a mess?

I remembered the time two summers ago when I got lost in the bush. I wandered around not knowing where I was going for about three or four hours, and then all at once I found our camp again. People say that's what happens sometimes in the bush, you just go in a big circle. It was kind of funny in a way 'cause when I got back, nobody even asked me where I had been. Nobody knew that I had been lost. They all figured that I was just out going for a walk or something. And I never told what happened either—I was too ashamed.

This time was different. Mave and I were together in the middle of a big city with hundreds of other people around us. We knew exactly where we were—at the Eaton Centre—but we were more lost than I had been that time all by myself in the bush. Crazy, eh?

CHAPTER SIX

I saw this mask once, half of it was painted red and the other half was black. On the red half, the mouth and the eyes were smiling and the face looked happy. But on the black half the mouth was twisted down in a frown and the whole expression was ugly and sad. Gok'mis said that the mask showed the good and the bad that's in everybody.

Toronto was like that mask. The red, happy side was the Eaton Centre where everybody was dressed nice and went around spending lots of money on clothes and food and stuff. The black, sad side was an old lady on the street about two blocks away.

She was sleeping on this plastic crate right on the sidewalk, snoring really loud. Her head was tipped back and her mouth was open so you could see she didn't have hardly any teeth. The weirdest thing about her was that she was wearing green plastic garbage bags for clothes. She probably had other clothes underneath, but on top all you could see was sort of a poncho and pants made of garbage bags. Her hair was long and gray and sticky-looking and her hands and face were all dirty. Around her on the sidewalk were about ten plastic shopping bags stuffed full of more crumpled plastic bags. I couldn't figure out what she wanted all those bags for.

The awful part was how the people on the street were just walking past like she was invisible—nobody even looked in her direction. Maybe they thought if they pretended that she wasn't there long enough, she might really disappear. I don't know.

Mave and I decided that she probably didn't have any place to live. I mean, why else would she be sleeping out there on the street? Lucky it was summer and warm out, but what did she do in the winter? And how come her family wasn't taking care of her? Everybody has a family. Maybe this lady had a son or a daughter somewhere who right that minute was watching TV or eating lunch in a fancy house. It just wasn't fair. I wished we had some food to give her, but we didn't.

And she wasn't the only one either. Where we were walking, especially in this park we came to, there were lots of people like her, most of them men though. Their clothes were all dirty and torn and they didn't have proper shoes. Some of them looked like they were drunk or crazy or maybe both. This one guy was yelling really loud to somebody beside him on the park bench—except nobody was there! But the guy, he acted like that imaginary person was so real that he made you feel like *you* were the crazy one 'cause you couldn't see the person, not him. It was creepy.

A couple of the men in the park were Indians. I could tell Mavis noticed them, but she didn't say anything. I guess they made her feel kind of funny too.

Mave and I didn't know where we were or where we were going. We just kept walking. We couldn't think of anything else to do. We had left the real downtown part of the city where the tall buildings and big stores were and now we were on streets with mostly houses. Some of them were fixed up really fancy, but lots were all messy and run-down. We started seeing "Old Cabbagetown" on the streetsigns.

"Hey! Cabbagetown—what's that?" Mave asked me. "We're not even in Toronto any more?"

"I don't know...we gotta be." I didn't really think we could have walked to another city already, but I decided to check anyway. There was a skinny black kid with a bike waiting to cross the street, so I went up to him. "Hey, is this Toronto?" I asked.

He looked at me as if I was crazy as that man in the park. "No, *you're* on the moon!" he said and he rode away.

I must have had a pretty stupid look on my face 'cause Mave giggled. "That means we're still in Toronto, eh Tafia?"

I had to smile too. It felt good. "Yup."

We sat down to rest on a bench in this big glass booth. "Now what?" Mave said.

"I don't know." My feet were starting to hurt and I was really hungry. We hadn't even eaten breakfast that morning, and now it was probably way past lunch already!

"I'm starving!" Mave said. I nodded.

Suddenly we heard a loud honk and there was a bus right in front of us waiting with the door open. The driver was waving us over. We realized then we were sitting at a bus stop. We shook our heads "no" and the door closed and the bus drove off again.

"C'mon," I said, "we can't stay here."

Mavis looked one way down the street and then the other. "Which direction should we go this time?"

"Oh, what's the difference?" I said.

She picked a street and we started walking

again. But Mavis got lucky this time 'cause a few minutes later we saw a sign on a red brick building that said: *Free Lunch 12 to 2. All Welcome.* That was for us! We followed the arrows to a room in the basement. All the way down the stairs we could smell the food. Boy did my stomach get excited!

The lady behind the counter looked surprised when she saw us. "C'mon kids, beat it."

"The sign says free lunch," Mavis answered. "We're hungry."

"It's not for kids." She pointed at the rows of tables and benches behind us. Sure enough there weren't any kids—only people like those we saw in the park.

"But we're hungry. It didn't say no kids," I said.

The lady shrugged but she didn't make any move to give us food. It looked like some kind of chicken and peas and potatoes, and there was lots of it left too.

"Aw, go on, Muriel, break your heart. Give them some." A guy had just come out of the kitchen carrying a big tray of glasses. He had black hair down to his shoulders and a big friendly smile. I was sure he was Indian. "It's nice to see some kids down here for a change," he said giving us a wink.

"Well...o.k...." Muriel agreed and she slopped some food on a couple of plates and handed them to us. She wasn't what you call a friendly type.

We thanked her and we went over the guy who had helped us. He was carrying a couple of big glasses of milk. "Here you go," he said. "Service with a smile." Then he sat down with us. "I'm Frank. Who're you?"

"She's Tafia and I'm Mavis," Mave said. Lucky one of us wasn't shy.

"Glad to meet you," Frank said and he shook hands with us. "Now go on, eat up! Don't mind me."

So we did, or at least we started to, but one mouthful of that chicken was enough. Mave and I looked at each other and we both made a face. It was gross! That guy Frank, he burst out into the loudest laughing. He was worse than Cheemo! I thought he'd fall off the bench.

"That's Muriel's best recipe too," he managed to say when he calmed down a bit. "Sickin-chicken I call it. That woman is the worst cook in the whole world! I heard she learned to cook at the zoo."

Well, maybe he thought it was funny, but for us it was no joke. It was either eat this awful stuff or be hungry.

"Say, how come you two girlies are down here anyway, mooching free grub? Don't your folks feed you at home?"

Mave and I started telling him all about what happened, but as soon as we said that we lived in

Spirit Bay he stopped us, all excited. "Spirit Bay! I know Spirit Bay! I spent a whole summer up there five...maybe six years ago. I was working, fishing with some friends. Best summer of my life! Ahh, what was the name of that guy up there.... I'm sure you must know him, he's real crazy—"

"Cheemo!" we both said together, laughing.

"Right! Cheemo, that was it," Frank said chuckling.

"He's my uncle," Mavis said.

"Mine too," I added.

"Is that right? Isn't that something! It's a small world, isn't it?"

It turned out he knew everybody—Aunt Lily, Baba, Mave's parents too. About every two seconds he'd say, "It's a small world!" like he just couldn't believe his good luck meeting up with us. It was nice.

When we'd finished our story, Frank shook his head. "So you never caught that kid, eh...the one who took the painting?" We shook our heads. "Well, that's the city for you. It's easy to lose people—even yourself if you're not careful...." He had kind of a faraway look on his face for a minute and then he was back with us. "Well, now, the first thing we do is call your father, Tafia. He'll know where Lily's friend lives. She probably even left the phone number with him."

But when we called there was no answer. "We'll try again later," Frank said. "Meantime we got to get some real food into you two skinnies."

He gave us some money and sent us over to a restaurant across the street. "That's where I always eat," he explained. "Just tell 'em Frank sent you."

It felt great having someone taking care of us again. I was sure we'd be back with Aunt Lily soon. She must've been worried to death by now.

CHAPTER SEVEN

The place Frank sent us was weird—extra weird. First of all, the only things you could get there were tacos, burritos, and enchiladas. That's what it said on the sign painted on the wall. Well, I guess if you live in the city you know that's Mexican food, but Mave and I sure didn't. Anyway, the guy behind the counter came over and asked what we wanted, so Mave just said two tacos. We didn't know what we were getting, so what was the difference what we ordered, right?

Then the guy asked, "Hot sauce?" We gave him two blank looks. He tried again. "You want hot sauce on your tacos?"

Mave shrugged. "Yeah, sure. I guess so. What do you think, Tafia?"

"Sure." Hot, cold, I didn't care, as long as it was food.

While we were waiting for our food we noticed

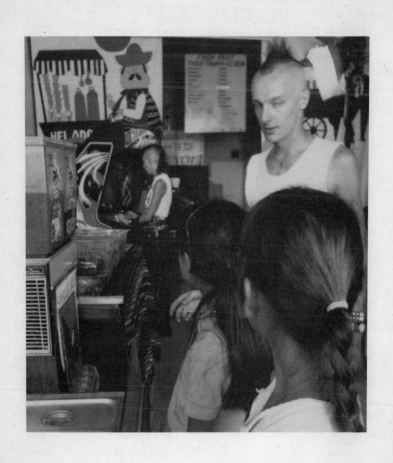

the second weird thing about this place. All the people hanging around in the back eating and playing video games were punk rockers. I'd seen punkers on TV, but these guys were weirder—'cause it was real life, I guess.

"Hey, look at him!" Mave said poking her elbow in my ribs. There was one guy who had a Mohawk hair cut—you know, all shaved except for a stripe of hair running from his forehead to the back of his neck. It wasn't a regular Mohawk though, it was all long and sticking out like a porcupine.

He must have noticed us watching him 'cause he came over. "Hey, I like that!" he said and he went to pick up Aunt Lily's painting.

I wasn't taking any chances on that painting getting stolen again, so I grabbed it and told him not to touch it. He lifted up his hands and backed away. "Hey, relax," he said. Then I felt bad, but how could I trust somebody who looked like that?

The guy behind the counter brought us our tacos. They smelled good so I took a huge bite. Boy was I sorry!! My mouth felt like it was on fire and my eyes started watering and I got really hot. I swallowed fast but the burning didn't go away.

"Hey, Gene," the punker called to the waiter, "I think the little girl needs some water."

I gulped down the water but it didn't make me feel any better. When I could talk again, I thanked him for his help. "Sure, no problem," he said. He had a nice friendly smile and he didn't seem so weird once you got used to him. He sat down with us.

"Why is your hair like that?" Mave asked him. I couldn't believe she said that, but he didn't get mad.

"Like what?" he said running his hand along his Mohawk.

"You know."

"I like it, I just like it."

"It looks weird. Anyway, Indians don't have hair like that," Mave told hm.

"How do you know? Are you an Indian?"

Before we could answer Frank came in the door of the restaurant and spotted us. "Hey, is this freak bothering you two girls?" he yelled picking the punker up under his arms. He sounded mad.

"No! No!" Mave and I shouted.

"Frank, my man, will you kindly put me down," the punker said giving Frank a friendly bop on the head. They knew each other—thank goodness!

We told Frank about our tacos. "Looks like this is not your day for food, eh?" he said sympathetically.

"So isn't anybody going to introduce us?" the punker asked. "I'm Bill."

"Her name is Tafia, and I'm Mavis," Mave said. "We're here to go to the powwow."

"A powwow? You're kidding!" Bill laughed. "You mean like smokum the peace pipe and heap big rain dance and all that jazz?"

"Don't tease the girls, Bill!" Frank told him.

"Hey, I was only kidding. Sorry." And he did look sorry. "You know Frank, I never think of you as being an Indian."

"Yeah, I know," Frank said. "I forget it myself sometimes."

"What do you do at a powwow anyway?" Bill asked us.

"Dance...and meet people," Mavis explained.

"Man, I love to dance! My girlfriend and I go out to Dominos all the time to dance. Watch this!" The best way to describe Bill's dancing was that he looked sort of like a chicken on a pogo stick.

"So...what do you think?" Bill said when he was finished.

"Show him what you do, Tafia," Mave said. "She's going to do the jingle dance at the powwow in front of everybody." And she gave me a funny look. I knew she was doing it on purpose—it was like a challenge. She hadn't forgotten what I'd said at the gas station about the powwow.

"No..." I said.

"Go on," Bill said. "I showed you mine. I'd love to see it."

"Yeah, me too," Frank agreed.

"No!!" I yelled. "I don't want to!"

Frank and Bill looked at each other kind of surprised. I guess they had figured I was the quiet type. They didn't know the whole story of Bone, the stubborn one—what my Gok'mis calls me.

After that we called Baba again and this time he was home. He sounded worried when I told him about being lost, but then Frank got on the phone and everything was o.k. again. That Frank is a fast talker! He got Monica's address from Baba too.

Before we left the restaurant, Bill bought us all tacos—*without* the hot sauce this time. They were sort of like Bill—o.k., once you got used to them.

CHAPTER EIGHT

I knew that the minute Aunt Lily saw us she would start crying—and sure enough, she did. What I didn't know was that I would be crying too. It was so good to see her face!

"Where were you?" she asked. "I was so scared. I didn't know where to look. I got as far as the subway but then I lost you. I went to the police. I've been on the phone all day. Oh I'm so glad you're both o.k.!" When Aunt Lily gets excited she never stops talking.

I showed her the painting. "Look, we got it back for you."

"Oh . . . you two!"

Finally she stopped hugging and crying over us long enough to look up and notice Frank. "Hi, Lily," he said shyly.

"Frank? Frank Raven, is that you?"

"Yup, it's me all right."

"Well, that's amazing! Frank! I can't believe it."
Aunt Lily went over and gave him a hug too. "And
you found these two and brought them back here."
She shook her head. "Well, it's sure a small world
isn't it."

"That's just what I was telling them," Frank said
with a silly grin.

"Well, let's go in and have a cup of coffee and
you can tell me all about it," and she hugged us all
over again. "Oh, what the heck! Let's have a
party—a party for Frank!"

Monica's place was upstairs. To get to it we had
to go through the art gallery. Frank stopped in
front of one of the paintings. "This is yours, isn't it,
Lily?"

You could see on Aunt Lily's face she was surprised that he recognized it, and pleased too.
"Yeah, how'd you know? My work has changed a
lot since the last time we met."

"Oh, I don't know," Frank said. "Maybe just a
lucky guess. It's good. I always liked your stuff."

"Thanks."

Frank didn't seem to want to leave the painting.
"This reminds me of home. Sure miss the bush."

"Why'd you leave?"

"Oh, I don't know. . . greener pastures. Anything
seemed better than the reserve back then. A guy
offered me a job in his garage here in Toronto,

fixing cars. He started acting funny—like he owned me or something. So I quit."

"What are you doing now?" Aunt Lily asked.

"Oh . . . I'm maître d' at a fancy restaurant."

Aunt Lily looked surprised. "Really?"

He shook his head with a grin. "No, I'm kidding. I work in this soup kitchen—that's where I met

Tafia and Mavis. Some job, eh? Food Social Worker, I call it."

"You could come back, you know...to the reserve."

"Yeah. I guess." Frank sounded kind of sad and lost. I noticed Aunt Lily was watching him closely. Concentrating. I guess she was thinking the same thing I was.

"Why don't you come to the powwow with us?" I asked Frank.

He scratched his head. "Well...I don't know." But I could tell he wanted to say yes.

Aunt Lily could too 'cause she said, "Sure. You could ride with my friend Monica. She's got lots of room. What do you say?"

Frank nodded slowly. "Well...maybe."

Before he left that night Frank promised to meet us on Friday at the powwow. Mave said she wasn't sure he'd show up. She made me a little mad. "He'll come, won't he?" I asked Aunt Lily.

"I hope so," she said. "Going to the powwow might help him."

"How do you mean?" Mave asked.

"Well, it's kind of like when you look all over the house for your hat and get really frustrated and then find it was on your head all along. That's sort of what Frank's doing now. Know what I mean?"

"Sort of," I answered. I guess Frank's trying to

figure out where he belongs. Just like Aunt Lily had to before she came back to live in Spirit Bay. "The city's no place for Indians, eh Aunt Lily?"

"Oh, I wouldn't exactly say that Tafia. Look at Monica—she's happy here. She helps to run this gallery, and she's doing fine. Everybody's different, that's all. Everybody has to find the way that's best for them."

"I'll never leave Spirit Bay," Mavis said.

"Me either." But I didn't feel as sure as Mave sounded.

"Well...we'll see," Aunt Lily said. "You never know what the future will bring."

"But I *do* know!" Mave said fiercely. "I'll never change my mind!" She was so serious, almost angry. Aunt Lily looked at her surprised, but I understood. It's on account of her family, her mother mainly. She wants her kids to be modern, move away from the reserve when they grow up. Mave always says how upset that makes her.

I remember when we were little and she used to ask Gok'mis to tell us those old stories about Windigo and Nanabush and all them. She didn't have anyone at home to tell her that stuff and she missed it.

But me, I thought Aunt Lily was right. How can you make up your mind for your whole life?

Mave and I had wasted one whole day in Toronto

being lost but we sure made up for it. In the next two days we did almost all the things we'd been planning. Aunt Lily was so glad to get us back, she went a little crazy, spoiling us.

Mave liked the CN Tower best—of course! Can you believe it, she wanted us to *walk* all the way up it! She said taking the elevator would be cheating. Lucky for Aunt Lily and me, they don't let you walk, it's against the rules. That's probably 'cause you'd get a heart attack doing it or something. That Mave!

CHAPTER NINE

The day we were leaving Toronto for the powwow, there I was again lying in bed in the early morning dark, my eyes wide open. That other morning, the one we left Spirit Bay, seemed like it was years back. So much had happened to me since then, everything seemed different—everything that is except the same old pain in my stomach and those mixed-up feelings. I had left the jingle dress at home—but here it was still haunting me.

I got up as quietly as I could so as not to disturb Mavis, and went down into the art gallery. I found the switch and turned on the lights so I could see the paintings. There was this one of Aunt Lily's that stopped me cold when I got to it. It was of a woman standing cooking some fish over a fire. She had on a beautiful sky-blue shawl with a yellow diamond pattern on the back. You couldn't see her face but you could tell she was old by the way her back was bent over. The person who bought that painting would never know who that old woman was, but I did. It was my Gok'mis.

As I stared at the back of her head I felt almost as if she had turned away from me on purpose. All of a sudden, more than anything in the world, I wanted to see Gok'mis' face. I felt in my heart that if I could just see her and talk to her that everything would be all right. "Gok'mis, please turn around," I begged. "Please turn around and look at me."

My voice echoed back at me, strange and spooky in the empty gallery.

"Gok'mis!" I said again.

"Tafia, what are you doing?"

I spun around to see Mavis standing in the doorway in her pyjamas, rubbing her eyes sleepily. Did she ever scare me! For just one second there I thought . . . .

"How come you're up already?" Mave asked. "It's so early." Then she was quiet for a second. "Umm. Tafia . . . can I ask you a question?"

I figured I already knew what her question was and there was no way I wanted to answer it. "No!!" I said.

"Tafia!" she said, starting to get mad. "Don't be

like that! I just want to ask you about your dancing. You're going to do it, aren't you? You're not going to chicken out are you?"

Now I was mad too. "It's not chickening out! Anyway I can't...I don't have my dress." I don't really know why I told her. I had kept it to myself all this time.

"What do you mean you don't have it?" Mave yelled, her voice going all high and squeaky.

"I left it at home."

"On purpose? Or did you forget it?"

I shrugged. "It's at home, that's all." I was trying to act like I didn't really care, but that just made Mave even madder.

"Tafia, sometimes you are so stupid!!"

"I am not! Don't call me that!"

"Hey, what's going on here? Yelling so early in the morning?" It was Aunt Lily. She looked back and forth between the two of us. I sure wasn't going to say anything, and to my surprise, Mave didn't either. I couldn't believe it—I was positive she'd tell on me.

"Come on. What is it?" Still no answer, so Aunt Lily gave up.

"O.k., o.k....but no more, all right? Let's all go get some breakfast."

While we were eating Mave and I didn't have too much to say to each other, or in the truck once we

71

got on the road. We hardly ever fight, but when we do it's serious. She usually gets things started and I'm stubborn, so that keeps them going. Like I told you before—Dog and Bone. I couldn't figure out why she was bugging me so much about the dancing. And why wouldn't she listen to me when I tried to explain how I was feeling? Mave just isn't like that most of the time. It was weird. Anyway, I had plenty to think about without worrying about her too. Things were getting pretty complicated.

I was sorry to be leaving Toronto, but when we got away from the city it was nice to see the fields and the woods and the lakes again—the real land. You know, if somebody came to visit Canada and just stayed in Toronto, they wouldn't know anything at all about what it's really like here—how wide and empty and free it is. And so big—lots of room for a person to spread out. Room for sitting quiet and thinking. That's one thing about the city—I don't know how anybody can do any good thinking there—it's so noisy and busy.

When we were about half-way to Curved Lake the trouble started. Old Band of Noises had been behaving so well the whole time in Toronto that it must have figured it was about time to raise a fuss. A flat tire—and with no spare!

We flipped a coin to decide which direction to go for help and then we started walking. When we finally got to a gas station the towtruck was out on another job, so we had to wait around. The guy kept telling us that they'd be there any minute, but we ended up sitting for over two hours. Aunt Lily finally borrowed a deck of cards and she tried to get us to play Crazy Eights or something, but Mave didn't want to. So Aunt Lily ended up sitting playing Solitaire while Mave and I tried hard to ignore each other. By the time the towtruck came, Aunt Lily was about ready to jump out of her skin she was so anxious to get going. Me, I could have hung out there forever. Or anyway till the pow-wow was over and I was safe.

"By the time we get there I bet we'll miss the grand entry," Aunt Lily said when we were rolling again. "I guess you'll have to wait till tomorrow to dance, Tafia. Sorry." Mave gave me a dirty look, but Aunt Lily didn't catch it—she was already at the powwow in her head. "The grand entry is so special. It starts at dusk, just when the sun goes down. Everybody gets very quiet and then the drummers start beating—really slowly at first. Then the dancers come into the circle, after the elders of course. It's so beautiful, everybody in their costumes: the men in their feather bustles and headdresses and fancy leggings and the women in their beaded buckskin dresses and those shawls with the long silky fringes. And then the singing starts and the dancing and it's wonderful!" Aunt Lily's eyes were glistening like she had tears in them. She's so emotional.

"You really think we'll miss it?" Mave asked.

"I'm afraid so, honey," Aunt Lily answered and she gave the dashboard a hard whack. "All on account of this stupid truck! We'll probably get to see some of the dancing tonight." She smiled at me. "And then of course tomorrow, when you get to dance, Tafia.... You know, I was talking to Monica's friend, Sal, about you. She's one of the organizers of the powwow. Sal said you'd probably be the only jingle dress dancer there. Nobody does it this far south. They might even ask you to dance by yourself—wouldn't that be great!?"

I didn't answer.

Mavis gave me another one of those looks when Aunt Lily said that. I almost wished she'd tell on me and get it over with so she wouldn't keep acting like this.

Well, I was sorry to miss the grand entry, but I sure wasn't sorry that my dancing was put off till the next day. I still didn't know what I was going to tell Aunt Lily about the jingle dress not being there. But one thing was for sure: Aunt Lily was going to be disappointed in me. It made me feel sick just thinking about it. Dancing would have been a

whole lot easier than having to tell Aunt Lily that I didn't have the dress.

It turned out that Aunt Lily was right—by the time we arrived, the dancing had already started. We could hear the drums and the chanting when we were still a long distance away. I got the shivers up and down my back, it sounded so spooky coming out of the dark like that.

We parked the truck and went over to watch. I had never seen so many Indians, and not just Ojibway and Cree, but Blackfoot and Iroquois, Navaho and Shawnee. So many faces, so many people. Right in the middle of the dancing area, this kind of roof covered with green branches had been set up—Aunt Lily called it an arbour. Under it all the drummers—I counted ten of them—were sitting in a circle around a huge drum. "I think it's the Eagle Singers," Aunt Lily whispered. "They're good!"

They were too. This one voice that seemed to be leading the other singers was really high and strong. I couldn't understand the words though, they were in some other language.

All around the arbour were the dancers, moving in circles, whirling, dipping, twirling, feathers and shawls flashing. There were lots of fancy dancers. You've probably seen them in pictures or movies.

They wear long feather headdresses and big feather bustles and fancy leggings. Their whole bodies are covered with decorations. And they dance so wild—I love them.

The beat of the drum started to get faster and faster and so did the dancers. It made me dizzy watching them. The colours of their costumes, red and blue and yellow and orange, all swirled together as they moved.

The whole thing was like magic. The drum beats and the singers' voices sounding like they were coming from long, long ago, from when Gok'mis was young or even before. And the dancers, like enchanted spirit birds out of a dream.

I looked at Mave and Aunt Lily standing beside me. They both had these happy grins on their faces—like a couple of excited little kids at a fair or something. And that's exactly what I was feeling like too.

I could almost feel the ground shaking under me from all those dancing feet. And you know what? I wanted to be out there too. Dancing to those magic drums, my whole body jingling, jingling, jingling....

Aunt Lily pointed to two little kids who were near us with their mother. One of them was still in diapers, but they were both jumping around laughing and clapping their hands. Were they ever cute.

"They're dancing, eh?" Aunt Lily said to their mother.

"Yeah," she answered with a smile. "Their dad's out there. Those two are going to be dancers too someday."

Aunt Lily put her arm around me and squeezed me tight. "Tomorrow, Tafia!" she whispered in my ear. "Tomorrow it'll be your turn."

But I knew she was wrong.

CHAPTER TEN

It was late by the time we found our camping spot. Putting up a tent is tricky anytime, but in the middle of the night with only the light of a campfire and a flashlight, it's *really* hard! We were too tired even to kill the mosquitos buzzing around inside the tent before collapsing into our sleeping bags.

We were sorry the next morning though. I had five bites and Mave had six—but Aunt Lily beat us both with thirteen! A swim in the river after breakfast made us forget all about them though.

We headed over to the crafts area where Monica had a stand, selling the silver jewellery she makes. Aunt Lily wanted to say hello—and check up on Frank. As we walked along the dusty road through the campgrounds, we saw cars with licence plates from all over—Manitoba, Quebec, Alberta, Michigan, New York. There was even one from the Northwest Territories that was in the shape of a polar bear. It was neat. Aunt Lily said she thought this might be the biggest powwow of the summer in all of Ontario.

There were paintings and pottery, beadwork, moccasins, carvings, blankets, all kinds of stuff for sale. And food! I'd just finished breakfast, but that corn soup and fried bread we saw made me wish it was lunchtime already.

We found Monica but when Aunt Lily asked about Frank, she shrugged and said, "He didn't show, Lily, sorry. I told him when I was leaving... What could I do?"

"Maybe he got a ride with somebody else," Monica added when she saw the disappointed look on Aunt Lily's face.

"Yeah, maybe..." Aunt Lily said.

"Some people, they just don't care about pow-wows and stuff," Mavis said. She didn't look at me, but I knew she wasn't just talking about Frank!

We hung around at Monica's stand for a while. It was so nice being there with all the people walking by, talking, joking, meeting friends; and the kids running and playing around—everybody having a good time. Then Aunt Lily bought some food for us to take back to our tent for lunch.

We were cleaning up when Aunt Lily said, "Tafia, you better get your dress on. It's almost time for the dancing."

The moment had finally come. I couldn't escape any longer.

I went slowly inside our tent and opened my bag

and sat down in front of it. I even checked inside, way at the bottom, to see if by some miracle the dress might be there. Pretty stupid eh, how you do things like that sometimes? Then I just sat there feeling miserable, not knowing what to do next.

Aunt Lily stuck her head into the tent. "Hey, what's taking so long?"

I swallowed hard and then the lies came tumbling out. "My dress, Aunt Lily...it isn't here...I guess I forgot it at home.... I'm sorry." And I burst into tears. I wasn't acting either, if that's what you're thinking.

"Oh, Tafia!" Aunt Lily said and she came over and put her arms around me and hugged me tight. "It's o.k. You don't have to cry...it's o.k." But her hugging me like that just made things worse instead of better.

You know how it is sometimes when you start crying and you keep thinking of more and more things to be sad about. Well that's what was happening to me. I thought about Aunt Lily being a little girl crying at night in her bed at that school, and I thought about Frank who was lonely in the city not being where he wanted to be, and I thought about Gok'mis who had been so proud about my dancing and how I was letting her down. And Mave being mad at me. And the Indian cowboy in Buffy Ste. Marie's song. There seemed to be so many sad things in the world and I was crying about all of them. It was terrible—my sadness was like a snowball rolling down a snowy hill getting bigger and bigger as it went. What I was mostly crying about though was me, Tafia—because now I wanted to dance and I couldn't.

"Tafia. It's o.k.," Aunt Lily said again, patting and rubbing my back just like I was a little baby. "Everybody forgets things sometimes. It's not the end of the world."

I felt so awful, her being so nice to me. I couldn't keep up my lies one more second. "But I didn't... *forget* it I mean," I sobbed. "I *left* it in the closet..."

Aunt Lily put her hands on my shoulders and looked at me all confused. She didn't really understand what I was saying.

"She left it home on purpose...because she didn't want to dance." Mavis was standing in the doorway of the tent. And she was staring right at me—through me, it felt like.

"What?! Why Tafia? Why?" Aunt Lily asked.

Why hadn't I brought my dress along to the powwow when everyone was looking forward to seeing me dance? I couldn't even remember my reasons any more. Why? Why? Why?

"I don't know...Mave is right...I'm just a chicken...I'm not good enough—"

"That's not what I said," Mave said angrily, "and

you know it!! I never said you weren't good enough."

"I know," I said. "None of the other kids were doing it, Aunt Lily! It was only 'cause Gok'mis—I never wanted to—"

"I would have done it!" Mave said, her voice choking up. "But I didn't have a dress or anything.... It's not fair!" And she started crying.

Now I knew why she had been bugging me so much about the dancing—'cause her parents would never let her do it. I was dancing in her place and now she didn't even have that. Poor Mave. I was worrying about letting down Gok'mis and Aunt Lily and everybody, but I never even thought about her. I felt like I didn't deserve her for a friend. I put my arm around her and she gave me a wet smile.

"But Tafia," Aunt Lily said, "Gok'mis didn't want you to dance for *her*. That wasn't what she wanted at all. Don't you understand that?"

I nodded. I didn't know then, but I did now. Gok'mis wanted me to dance for *me*.

"You're just like I was, making the same mistakes, turning your back on—"

"Oh no Aunt Lily!!" I said. "I'm not...I've changed my mind.... I want to dance. If I had my dress here, I'd wear it. I really would!!" I really wanted her to believe me, and she did.

"It's o.k. Tafia, it's o.k."

Suddenly we heard someone yelling outside. We looked at one another and smiled. There was only one person a voice that loud could belong to.

"Cheemo!!" we all shouted.

"You guys still sleeping in there or what?" he was calling. "Hey, you'll never guess who came—" We came out of the tent to a big welcoming smile. "That's better! I have arrived. So let the dancing begin."

Aunt Lily went over and gave Cheemo a big kiss, and Mave and I tried to too but he just attacked us with tickling. Some people never change! Thank goodness, I guess, if they're Cheemo.

"So tell us," Aunt Lily said, "who's here?"

"What?" Cheemo scratched his head. "Did I say somebody was here?" He tried to look innocent, but there was a twinkle in his eye.

"Chee-mo!" Aunt Lily warned. "If you don't tell us right now.... Was it Frank Raven?"

"Frank who—?" But before he got any further the three of us had him down on the ground, Mave sitting right on his stomach. It was fun to be fooling around again. I could tell Mave and Aunt Lily were feeling the same way.

Just then I looked up to see somebody walking slowly along the trail toward our campsite. But it wasn't Frank....

It was my Gok'mis!

CHAPTER ELEVEN

I couldn't believe my eyes! Gok'mis!!

I was glad to see her, but I was scared too. She had come all this way to see me dance. How could I tell her what I had done?

"Oh yeah," Cheemo said turning to look. "I had a passenger on my trip down."

"I thought she didn't want to come," Aunt Lily said. "I asked her and she said no."

Cheemo shrugged. "All I know is, she came over the day you all left and said she wanted to go too. It was o.k. with me."

I left the others and ran to meet her. "Gok'mis! Gok'mis! You're here!"

"I'm here," she said in Ojibway, nodding and smiling at me. "I have come to see you dance."

I looked down at the ground and my eyes were swimming with tears. I was so ashamed.

Then I felt her put a paper bag into my hand.

"What?! What's this?"

She didn't answer.

I opened it and there was my dress. My beautiful turquoise jingle dress!

"Gok'mis!" I said hugging her. "Thank you for bringing it! How did you know? How did you find it?"

"You made a mistake," she said simply.

I was about to say that she was wrong, that it wasn't a mistake, but then I realized what she meant. I *had* made a mistake when I left the dress behind in my closet. And now Gok'mis was helping me to make that mistake right again. I had my dress and I was going to dance!

"Thank you," I said again. "You aren't mad?"

She shook her head. "You are learning to fly, like the young bird." Like always, Gok'mis didn't need any explanations. She could see that I had changed; that I wasn't the same Tafia who had left my dress behind in the back of my closet.

Then she held out her hand to me. It was her eagle feather. "For you," she said.

My heart felt like it would burst! You see, for our people, an eagle feather is a sacred thing. And when someone gives you one it's a great honour.

The feather was Gok'mis' way of saying that she was proud of me, that she trusted me to carry on our traditions.

"You will wear it now," Gok'mis said patting my shoulder.

I went back to the tent to get ready. Inside the bag with my jingle dress, I found my headdress and my dancing moccasins. Charlotte, Gok'mis' friend, had made the headdress for me. It was all covered with beads. There was a pattern of red and yellow flowers around it, and hanging down at the sides were two long pieces of soft white rabbit fur. I touched it to my face. Soft! The fur was for the kingdom of the animals; the flowers were for the kingdom of the plants.

Onto the back of my headdress I carefully fastened the eagle feather. It was important for it not to fall off while I was dancing. An eagle feather is never supposed to touch the ground. I remembered what had happened once when I saw a fancy dancer lose one of the eagle feathers in his bonnet. Suddenly all the dancing and drumming had stopped. Four elders came out and one of them picked up the feather. First they put tobacco where it had landed, and then the man who lost it gave them something in exchange to get it back, I couldn't tell what. I knew if the feather fell again that he would have lost it for good. Like I said, eagle feathers are sacred.

I was so proud that Gok'mis had given it to me. When I wore this feather I would be dancing for Gok'mis and for her mother and for her mother before her. And for all the others too—Mavis, Aunt Lily, Baba, Minnow, Cheemo, Frank—everybody! I wasn't just Tafia Shebagabow all by myself, I was part of something bigger—part of the Ojibway people. And I had something to bring to my people and to share with them—my dancing. I knew then that I would never again in my life forget who I was.

When I came out of the tent with my costume on, everybody was standing around outside waiting for me. They all said how nice I looked, but no one mentioned the feather. I knew that they had noticed it though, and that they were happy.

*　　*　　*

I am standing in the dancing circle under the hot sun. I can feel the drum beating in my feet and in my heart. The drummers are chanting, "Hay, yah, hay yah, hay yah hay..." I can see the people around me, the other dancers, leaping and kicking up the dust. A fancy dancer beside me is turning in circles, stamping his feet on the ground—fast, like the ruffed grouse in the spring calling for his mate. On the other side of me are two women with striped blankets over their shoulders turning slowly like leaves in a soft breeze. It's like in a dream, the drum beats coming at us like waves beating over and over again on the shore. "Hay yah, hay yah, hay yah hay..."

And past the dancers I see the others: my family and my friends smiling proudly. I feel sorry that Frank's face is missing from the crowd. Him being here too would make it perfect. I touch the eagle feather in my headdress and Gok'mis nods slowly to show that she understands. I know that the most important thing is that we're all here and we're all together.

I put my one hand on my hip and I begin to dance. Hop, hop, hop, three times on one foot; then hop, hop, hop, three times on the other foot. As I move, the jingles on my dress tinkle together and my whole body is turned into a beautiful instrument. I catch the beat of the drum in my feet. Hop, hop, hop; hop, hop, hop; hop, hop, hop. It's an old dance that I do. The dance of my people. I feel brave and strong and I'm flying. Flying! Flying like dancing feathers in the wind.

Christel Kleitsch was born in East Germany, but moved to Canada at age 3. She grew up in Montreal and attended the University of Toronto.

Christel says she likes to sleep, eat, read, see movies, skydive, drive racing cars, train mountain gorillas, explore tropical icebergs, translate ancient Byxtplruzian poetry into Aswallillian, and advise world leaders.

One of Christel's stories for children won the CBC Radio Literary Competition in 1984.

Don Ense grew up on Manitoulin Island in Ontario. He has worked as an artist for many years and is now a veteran of 45 group art exhibitions. In his work Don employs various media and techniques, ranging from pottery (ceramics) to acrylic paintings (fine art). His work has been exhibited in Canada, the United States and Europe and is on permanent display in several private and public collections.

In addition, Don has been featured in several native and non-native magazines, newspapers, art collections and books.